The Berenstain Bears and the MANSION MYSTERY

Stan & Jan Berenstain

HAPPY HOUSE BOOKS
Random House, Inc.

Copyright © 1987 by Berenstains, Inc. All rights reserved under International and Pan-American Copyright Conventions. Published in the United States by Random House, Inc., New York, and simultaneously in Canada by Random House of Canada Limited, Toronto. ISBN: 0-394-88901-0 Manufactured in the United States of America 1 2 3 4 5 6 7 8 9 0

One day Papa Bear, who made and repaired furniture, got a call from Squire Grizzly.

"The squire wants me to come over and talk about some business," said Papa. He was very pleased, because Squire Grizzly was the richest bear in Bear Country and would make a very good customer.

"May we come along, Unc?" asked Cousin Freddy, who was visiting.

"I hear Squire Grizzly has some great stuff in that mansion of his!" added Brother Bear.

"Please, Papa!" begged Sister Bear.

"Why not," said Papa.

"Wow!" said Freddy when the mansion came into view. "That's some place!"

"Yes," agreed Sister, "and look at the beautiful grounds!"

"Hey! Where are you going, Unc?" shouted Freddy as Papa steered around to the back. "There's the front door!"

"Lady Grizzly doesn't let *anybody* come in the front door," explained Papa, "not even Squire Grizzly.

"We're here to see Squire Grizzly," said Papa when Grizzby, the butler, answered their knock.

"I shall tell the master you are here," he said.

No sooner were they inside the mansion than they heard a scream. It was from Lady Grizzly.

"We've been robbed!" she wailed. "Someone has stolen three of my favorite things: my writing desk, my precious carved chest, and my adorable pepper mill—all valuable antiques."

"This," said Brother, "looks like a case for—"

"The Bear Detectives!" shouted Sister and Cousin Freddy.

Freddy went to the back door and did his special whistle. Quick as a wink his sniffer hound, Snuff, appeared carrying the Bears' detective kit in his mouth.

"Don't you worry, ma'am," said Brother. "The Bear Detectives are on the case!"

"*And* the world's greatest detective—Papa Q. Bear!" said Papa, who thought he was the world's greatest expert at just about everything.

"But, my good fellow..."
said the squire, taking
Papa aside.

"That reminds me, Squire.
What was it you wanted to
see me about?" asked Papa.

"That can wait. First,
I must—"

"You're right, Squire,"
agreed Papa. "Everything
must wait until we find the
thief! I believe he's still here.
These old mansions are tricky—
full of secret hiding places!

"Aha!" Papa cried. "A secret door! Concealing a secret passageway, no doubt! Cover me, Detectives! I'm going in!"

"You're covered, all right," said Sister, "by coats and hats!"

"That's not a secret passage, Unc!" added Freddy. "It's a clothes closet!"

"I told you this place was tricky," said Papa.

Snuff was already busy sniffing some little black grains in the area where the stolen things had been. Suddenly he sneezed.

Brother picked up some of the black grains and sniffed them. He sneezed too. "Ahchoo!"

"What is it?" asked Freddy.

"Don't know," answered Brother, inspecting it through his magnifying glass. "But whatever it is, it's an important clue."

"Nonsense," interrupted Squire Grizzly. "Those aren't clues but simply peppercorns which must have fallen from the stolen pepper mill."

"Oh, my lovely things!" wailed Lady Grizzly.

"Calm yourself, my dear," said the squire, helping her over to a large chair. "Sit here. I'll get you a glass of water."

Then, when nobody was looking, a very strange thing happened. The chair and wall began to move! It was a trick chair. Before Lady Grizzly knew what was happening, she disappeared into the wall.

"Ruff!" said Snuff, sniffing the floor.

"He's picked up the scent!" shouted Brother. "Sister, tell Lady Grizzly we're on the trail!"

Snuff pulled Brother to the door of a dark, spooky-looking room.

"This looks like the squire's trophy room," said Papa.

"Hold everything!" cried Sister. "Lady Grizzly has disappeared!"

"This is getting serious," said Freddy.

"I can't find Squire Grizzly or the butler, either," said Sister.

"Seriouser and seriouser," said Freddy as Snuff, still hot on the trail, pulled them into the trophy room. Three suits of armor with battleaxes seemed to guard the way.

"Ruff!" said Snuff, sniffing the trail. Then, once again, he sneezed. "Ahchoo!"

"I think Snuff may be catching cold," said Freddy. "This old mansion is pretty drafty."

"Hmm," said Sister. "I don't think so."

Snuff was working up another sneeze—a really big one. *"Ah-ah-ah-CHOO!"* It shook the whole room. It shook the battleaxes loose. Whomp!... Whomp!...Whomp! They fell, one right after the other.

"*Yipe!*" yelled Papa as he and the cubs raced out of the way. Then Snuff, still sneezing, led them outside to a dark, overgrown path leading to a shed.

"Look!" said Papa, peering through the window.
"The missing antiques!" And sure enough, there
they were—the desk, the chest, and the pepper mill.
"Hmm," he said. "They're fine pieces, all right,
but they're not in very good shape."

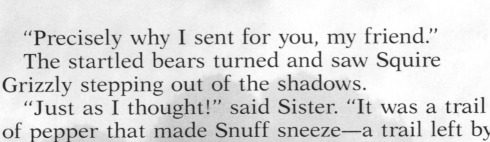

"Precisely why I sent for you, my friend."
The startled bears turned and saw Squire Grizzly stepping out of the shadows.

"Just as I thought!" said Sister. "It was a trail of pepper that made Snuff sneeze—a trail left by Squire Grizzly himself—probably through a hole in his pocket."

"By Jove!" said the squire. "I *do* have a hole in my pocket—and the pepper's all gone!"

"The pepper you removed from the pepper mill before you stole it!" accused Sister.

"Squire Grizzly," said Papa, "you're under arrest for stealing your own antiques!"

"Stuff and nonsense, dear chap!" Squire Grizzly protested. "I called you to repair Lady Grizzly's favorite things as a special birthday surprise. But she returned unexpectedly from a trip and upset my plans.

"Now, quickly! Load the things into your car and be off with you. Grizzby is fetching her from our secret passageway even now."

Papa and the cubs loaded the "stolen" antiques into the car and made a fast getaway.

"Happy birthday, my dear!" said the squire as he presented the beautifully repaired antiques to Lady Grizzly a few days later.

"What a lovely surprise!" Lady Grizzly said. "My precious things weren't stolen after all, merely spirited away for repairs. And thank you, Papa Bear—your repair work is excellent!"

"And the Bear Detectives' work is pretty good too," said the squire, chuckling. "A little *too* good!"

"Ruff!" said Snuff.